Grandpa on Holiday

ROB LEWIS

RED FOX

A Red Fox Book

Published by Random House Children's Books
20 Vauxhall Bridge Road, London SW1V 2SA

A division of Random House UK Ltd
London Melbourne Sydney Auckland Johannesburg
and agencies throughout the world

Copyright © Rob Lewis 1997

1 3 5 7 9 10 8 6 4 2

First published in Great Britain by Red Fox 1997

Printed in Hong Kong

RANDOM HOUSE UK Limited Reg. No. 954009

ISBN 0 09 921882 8

THE
BEACH HOUSE

Grandpa, Finley, Mum and
Dad were going on holiday.
They were driving to a house
by the sea.
Everyone was gloomy.
It was raining hard.
'I hope it doesn't rain all holiday,'
said Finley.
'I will tell a story to cheer us up,'
said Grandpa.

Grandpa told a scary story.

'A monster with bat wings bashed at the door,' said Grandpa, 'but the door was locked ...'

Finley looked out of the window.

The sky was getting darker and darker.

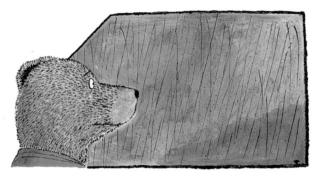

'So the monster went to the back door and turned the door handle,' said Grandpa, 'and the door opened ...'

Dad switched on the headlights.

'And the monster stomped up the stairs,' continued Grandpa, 'and opened the cupboard door...'

'This must be the beach house,' said Mum.

Dad stopped the car.

'I will get the key from the next house,' he said.

'I will come too,' said Mum. 'The beach house looks scary in the dark.'
'We're not scared!' said Grandpa and Finley. 'We will stay here.'
Grandpa and Finley sat in the car.

'Let's see if the beach house is open,'
said Grandpa.

'We should wait for Mum and Dad,'
said Finley.

'You're not scared, are you?' smiled
Grandpa.

'No,' said Finley.

They tried to open the front door.

It was locked.

'I will check the back door,'
said Finley.

The back door was open.

'I will play a trick on Grandpa,' said
Finley. 'Then we will see if Grandpa
is scared.'

Grandpa waited in the porch.

He heard a noise.

'Woooh!'

it went.

Grandpa was scared.

'I will look for Finley,' he said.

Grandpa went to the back door.

'Boo!'

said Finley.

'I wasn't scared,' said Grandpa.

'This is an old house,' said Finley.

'There are no lights.'

'I will find some candles,'
said Grandpa.

But Grandpa did not find any candles.

Instead he found a bag of flour.

'I will play a trick on Finley,' he said.

Finley was in the lounge.

He heard a noise upstairs.

'Grrrrrrr!'

it went.

Finley was scared.

He went upstairs to look.

'Boo!'

said Grandpa, jumping out of a
cupboard.

'I wasn't scared,' said Finley.

Suddenly someone banged on the
front door.
He could not get in.
'It's only Mum and Dad,' said Finley.
'But Mum and Dad have the keys!'
said Grandpa.
It was the monster with bat wings.

Grandpa *and* Finley were scared.

The monster went to the back door
and turned the handle.

The door opened.

Grandpa and Finley hid in the
cupboard.

The monster stomped up the stairs.

And opened the cupboard door ...

'Sorry to scare you,' said Dad.

'This is the wrong house. Our beach house is further down the road.'

'We weren't scared!'

trembled Grandpa and Finley.

STICKY PICNIC

It was a hot day.

'Let's have a picnic,' said Finley.

'Okay,' said Mum.

Mum made a cake.

Finley washed
some salad.

Grandpa made lots of
syrup sandwiches.
They were very sticky.

Dad drove everyone down to the beach.

Mum laid out the tablecloth.

Grandpa laid out the sandwiches.
The syrup sandwiches had made
everything sticky.

They started to eat. Flies buzzed
around the syrup sandwiches.

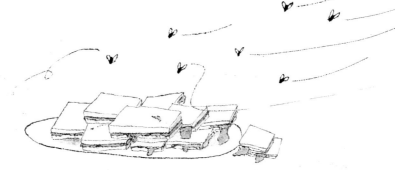

'Go away, flies,' said Finley.

Grandpa hit them with his newspaper.

He missed the flies and hit Mum's

cake.

Then gulls came to steal the syrup
sandwiches.

'Clear off, gulls,' said Dad.

Mum waved them away with a towel.
She missed the gulls but hit
Finley's lemonade.

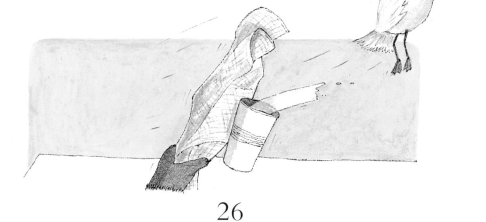

Then wasps flew around the sandwiches.

'Get lost, wasps!' shouted Grandpa.

Finley swiped at them with his hat.

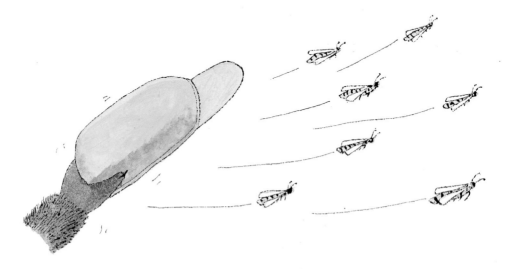

He hit one wasp but another stung Dad.

'Aaaah!'

yelled Dad.

'These sandwiches are trouble.'

'I will move them,' said Grandpa.

Finley mopped up his lemonade.

Mum cut the cake.

Dad nursed his wasp sting.

And Grandpa moved the sandwiches.

It started to rain.

'Oh no!' they all said. They picked up all the food and got in the car. Then they ate cake and watched the rain.

'At least we are dry,' said Grandpa.

'And there are no flies or gulls,' said Finley.

'Or wasps,' said Dad.

Mum looked down.

Something was crawling up her leg.

'Ants!' she said.

Mum looked at Grandpa.

'Where *did* you put those syrup
sandwiches?' she said.

'Um ...' said Grandpa, worriedly.
'I think you're sitting on them!'

THE AIR BED

Grandpa and Finley found a cove.

'You go and explore,' said Grandpa.

'I will stay here and sunbathe.'

'I want to sunbathe too,' said Finley.

'I will lie on the air bed,'

said Grandpa.

'You can lie on the stones.'

'But Mum said I could lie on the air

bed,' said Finley.

'I am old and creaky,' said Grandpa.

'I need a soft place to lie down.'

Grandpa pretended to be old

and creaky.

Finley didn't want to sunbathe on pebbles. He decided to explore the cove instead.

He looked under a stone and found a crab.

He looked in a rockpool and found a starfish and some long, green, slimy seaweed.

He put them in a bucket.

'Look, Grandpa,' said Finley.

Grandpa's eyes were closed.

'Very nice,' said Grandpa.

'I will look for more things,' said Finley.

'Don't go too far,' said Grandpa.

'The sea can be dangerous.'

Grandpa was very comfortable on the air bed. It was like floating on a cloud. Soon he was fast asleep.

But when he opened his eyes he found he was floating on water. The air bed had drifted out to sea.

Grandpa paddled towards the shore.
But a strong wind blew him further
out to sea.

Soon he could not see land.

he shouted.

The wind became stronger.

The waves grew bigger.

The clouds got darker.

Soon he was in the middle of a big storm. Thunder was rumbling across the sky. Waves were crashing over him and the air bed began to sink.

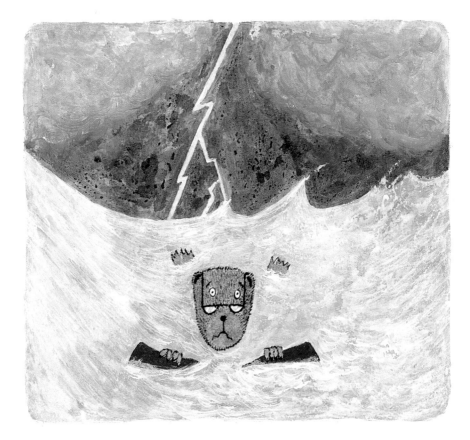

Suddenly out of the waves came long, green, slimy tentacles.

Then two big eyes and two big claws.

'Help!' cried Grandpa. 'A sea monster.'

'Sorry, Grandpa,' said Finley.

Grandpa woke up.

'My bucket fell over,' said Finley.

Finley took away the seaweed.

The crab scuttled away from Grandpa.

'I will put the crab and the starfish
back in the sea,' said Finley.
'You can go back to sleep now.'

'I have changed my mind,' said Grandpa. 'You can have the air bed and *I* will go and explore!'